S0-AFG-519

A World of Food

THE CARIBBEAN

Jen Green

CLARA
HOUSE
BOOKS

Minneapolis

First published in 2010 by Clara House Books, an imprint of The Oliver Press, Inc.

Clara House Books
5707 West 36th Street
Minneapolis, MN 55416, USA

Produced by Arcturus Publishing Limited

Series concept: Alex Woolf
Editor: Alex Woolf
Designer: Jane Hawkins
Map illustrator: Stefan Chabluk
Picture researcher: Alex Woolf

Picture Credits
Corbis: 4 (Bob Krist), 6 (Stapleton Collection), 8 (Bob Krist), 9 (Steve Raymer), 10 (Jean Louis Atlan/Sygma), 11 (Tony Arruza), cover and 15 (Stuart Westmorland), 17 (Howard Davies), 18 (Shepard Sherbell), 19 (Tony Arruza), 24 (Philip Gould), 29 (Tony Arruza).
Getty Images: 7 (Hulton Archive), 20 (Thony Belizaire/AFP), 23 (Bruce Dale/National Geographic), 27 (David Sanger/The Image Bank).
Rex Features: 12 (Neil Emmerson/Robert Harding), 22 (Eye Ubiquitous), 26 (Nico Tondini/Robert Harding), 28 (Charles Knight).
Shutterstock: 13 rice (Valentyn Volkov), 13 kidney beans (David William Taylor), 13 coconut (Olga Lyubkina), 13 red pepper (Serp), 13 green onions (Barbro Bergfeldt), 13 thyme (Drozdowski), 14 (Rohit Seth), 16 (Javarman), 21 allspice (oznuroz), 21 garlic (Iwona Grodzka), 21 chilli (Lagrima), 21 green onions (ultimathule), 21 raw chicken with jerk seasoning (Monkey Business Images), 21 jerk chicken with rice and peas (Rohit Seth), 25 mango (Danny Smythe), 25 orange juice (Sandra Caldwell), 25 pineapple (Alex Staroseltsev), 25 lime (Atronom), 25 fruit punch (FrankfurtDave).

Library of Congress Cataloging-in-Publication Data

Green, Jen.
The Caribbean / Jen Green.
        p. cm. -- (A world of food)
Includes bibliographical references and index.
ISBN 978-1-934545-15-7
1. Food habits--Caribbean Area. 2. Cookery, Caribbean. 3. Caribbean Area--Social life and customs. I. Title.
GT2853.C27G74 2010
394.1'2--dc22

                                                                    2009036248

Dewey Decimal Classification Number: 394.1'2'09729

ISBN 978-1-934545-15-7

Printed in China

www.oliverpess.com

Contents

Tropical Islands

The Caribbean is a group of islands in the Caribbean Sea, which lies between North and South America. There are about 30 large islands and thousands of smaller ones. The Caribbean is known for its clear blue seas, sandy beaches, sunny weather – and for its delicious cooking.

There are three main groups of Caribbean islands. The Bahamas are a group of small islands off the southeastern United States. To the south, the Greater Antilles include the four biggest islands in the Caribbean – Cuba, Jamaica, Hispaniola, and Puerto Rico. Hispaniola is divided between two nations, Haiti and the Dominican Republic. The Lesser Antilles lie to the east. They are divided into two groups – the Windward Islands, including Martinique, Dominica, Trinidad and Tobago, and the Leewards, including Guadeloupe, Montserrat, and St Kitts.

▲ A market stall in the Bahamas. Caribbean people like to cook with fresh produce bought daily from the market.

Lush conditions

The Caribbean enjoys a warm, wet, tropical climate. Fruit trees, crops, and many other plants grow well in these conditions. These islands were once covered in lush forests, but now there are many farms and plantations.

Many peoples

The Caribbean is often called a "melting pot" of people and cultures. People from South America, Europe, Africa, Asia, and the Middle East have all settled here over the centuries. All have brought their own traditions, including religious beliefs, music, and styles of cooking. This makes the Caribbean a very special place – and explains the wide range of tasty cooking you can sample on these islands.

▼ This map shows the Caribbean, also known as the West Indies.

FRESH FROM THE MARKET

Caribbean cooking includes an amazing range of dishes, but all have one thing in common – fresh ingredients. Many people visit the market daily to buy fresh fish, fruit, and vegetables. Tropical fruits such as bananas, pineapples, and mangoes are piled high on market stalls. Many of the market traders are women.

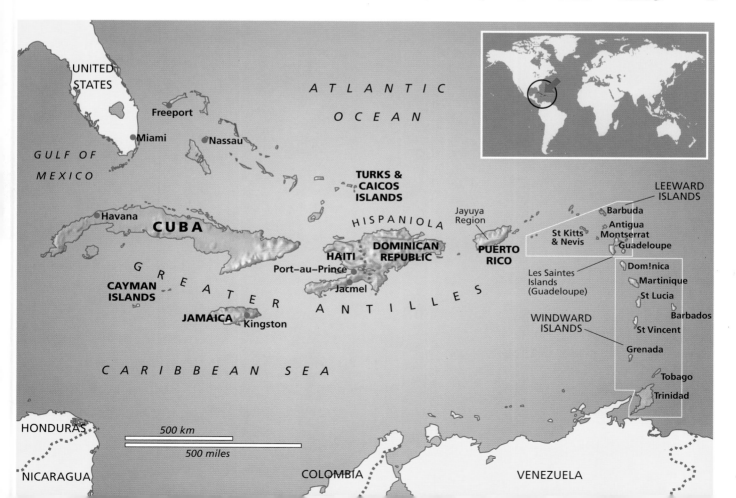

UNITED STATES
Freeport
Miami
Nassau
GULF OF MEXICO
ATLANTIC OCEAN
TURKS & CAICOS ISLANDS
Havana
CUBA
HISPANIOLA
Jayuya Region
LEEWARD ISLANDS
Barbuda
Antigua
St Kitts & Nevis
Montserrat
Guadeloupe
DOMINICAN REPUBLIC
HAITI
PUERTO RICO
Port-au-Prince
Les Saintes Islands (Guadeloupe)
Dom!nica
Martinique
CAYMAN ISLANDS
Jacmel
St Lucia
GREATER ANTILLES
Barbados
JAMAICA
Kingston
WINDWARD ISLANDS
St Vincent
Grenada
CARIBBEAN SEA
Tobago
Trinidad
HONDURAS
500 km
500 miles
NICARAGUA
COLOMBIA
VENEZUELA

Early History

The first inhabitants of the Caribbean were Native Americans from South America. About 500 years ago, Europeans arrived to colonize the islands. They introduced slaves from Africa and, later, workers from faraway Asia. Each group brought new customs and ways of cooking to the region.

▲ This old illustration shows the first meeting Christopher Columbus had with the Native Americans, in 1492.

The first peoples to settle the Caribbean included Arawaks and Caribs from South America. The Arawaks lived as farmers, growing crops such as sweet potatoes, cassava, peppers, and tobacco. They cooked meat by rubbing it with herbs and spices and grilling it over a barbecue. The Caribs lived by fishing as well as farming, and gave the Caribbean its name.

Conquest

In 1492, a Spanish expedition led by Christopher Columbus landed in the Caribbean. During the 1500s, many islands became Spanish colonies. In the 1600s, Britain, France, and Holland set up their own colonies. The Europeans conquered the Native Americans and enslaved them. Europeans also brought many new crops, including sugar cane, bananas, oranges, and coconuts. They set up plantations to grow these crops and tobacco for profit. Each European nation brought its own recipes and style of cooking.

Slavery

The Europeans forced Arawaks and Caribs to work on the plantations. But within a century or so, the original inhabitants had virtually been wiped out through overwork and disease. The Europeans began to ship slaves from West Africa to take their place. African slaves brought new foods such as okra, beans, and yams, and new spicy ways of cooking. Over the years, some islands changed hands among the Europeans, but the terrible conditions on the plantations did not change.

WHITE GOLD

Sugar cane was the most important crop in colonial times. It was so valuable it was called white gold. The ripe cane was cut by hand in the old days. Now it is mostly cut by machine. In the sugar mill, the cane is crushed to make juice. This is boiled to make a dark, thick syrup called molasses. The syrup is then processed to make sugar, and also rum.

▶ This illustration shows African slaves working on the sugar plantations. Some of the workers are children.

7

Free and Independent

Slavery continued through the 1600s and 1700s. When it finally ended, Asian workers replaced African slaves on the plantations. In the early 1900s, many islands struggled to gain independence, and yet more peoples arrived, including from the Middle East. They helped to create the amazingly varied cooking found in the Caribbean today.

Slaves suffered greatly even before they arrived on the plantations. They were packed into the stuffy holds of slave ships and many thousands died on the journey. Once on the plantations, slaves toiled from dawn to dusk, in constant fear of the overseer's whip. In the 1800s, after centuries of cruelty, slavery ended. Many ex-slaves became farmers, working small plots of land in the hills.

New workers

The Europeans now needed a new workforce. East Indian and Chinese people arrived to work for a certain number of years for low pay. Called indentured workers, they brought new customs – and new forms of cooking. The Indians brought rice, breads, and spicy curries.

▶ Indian dishes are served at a wedding on Trinidad, where 40 percent of people are of Indian descent.

The Chinese had their own flavors and recipes, which you can still sample in the Caribbean today.

Independence

In the early 1900s, many Caribbean countries pressed for independence. Meanwhile, new waves of settlers arrived in search of work. They included Jews, Portuguese, and immigrants from Syria and Lebanon. All added to the melting pot of Caribbean culture and cuisine.

After World War II ended, many nations across the globe won independence. There are now around two dozen island states in the region. Cuba and Haiti officially are republics. Islands such as Jamaica, Barbados, and the Bahamas are parliamentary democracies. Many maintain close links with the countries that once ruled them. Other islands, such as the United States Virgin Islands and Martinique, are still overseas territories.

▶ Indentured workers such as this man arrived to replace slave labor.

SOME COMMON FOOD TERMS

Many languages are spoken in the Caribbean. Some speak Creole, or patois – a mixture of European and African words. Here are a few common food words in Jamaican patois.

Word	Meaning
alligator pear	avocado
bulla	cookie
bammy	round cassava bread
chocho	squash similar to potato
coo-coo	mashed cornmeal
dukunu	sweet cornmeal dumpling
janga	crayfish
jelly	flesh of a young coconut
ital	pure, natural food
patty	pasty with a spicy filling
rundown	salt-fish stew
stamp and go	cod fritters

Climate and Soil

Temperatures are warm all year round in the Caribbean. Rainfall is generally plentiful, and the soil is fertile. All this makes the region ideal for farming. However, parts of the islands are too steep or stony for crops.

The Caribbean basks in tropical temperatures, which soar to 86°F degrees (30°C) in summer. In winter they only drop to around 73°F (23°C). Mountains are cooler, but still frost free. Moist winds called trade winds blow off the Atlantic Ocean, bringing rain. Many islands get most of their rain between June and November. Around the same time, hurricanes sometimes blow in from the ocean. These huge spinning storms can wreck farms and towns.

Land and soil

Most Caribbean islands were formed by movement of the giant rocky plates that make up the Earth's crust. Where two of these plates press together, the land between very slowly buckles upwards, forming mountains on the seabed. These eventually rise above the surface to form islands. Molten rock may surge upwards in the same areas to form volcanoes.

◄ Rice thrives in hot, wet conditions. It is grown in flooded fields called paddies, such as here on Haiti.

Many islands are the tips of underwater volcanoes. Some volcanoes are still active. In 1995, a volcano on Montserrat began erupting violently, and everyone had to leave the island.

Mountains and lowlands

Volcanic rock eventually wears away to form fertile soil for farming. However, the mountains in the center of many islands are too steep for farming. The best land is usually the fertile strip around the coast. In some places, steep hillsides are terraced – cut into little steps that make small, flat fields. Crops such as coffee thrive in the cool mountain air.

GROWING PLANTAINS

Plantains are an important crop, mostly grown on plantations in the lowlands. These are a type of banana that have to be cooked before they are eaten. Plantains are featured in many recipes. They are served boiled or fried as a side dish, or deep-fried to make tasty chips.

▼ Coffee is grown on these terraces in the mountains of Puerto Rico.

Food and Farming

A huge variety of crops are grown in the Caribbean. Some are native to the region. Others were introduced by European, African, or Asian settlers.

Rice, beans, and root vegetables such as sweet potatoes and cassava are staple foods in the Caribbean. Yams and breadfruit are baked, boiled, or fried instead of potatoes. Callaloo is a leafy vegetable like spinach. Tropical fruits thrive in the Caribbean, including bananas, mangoes, oranges, pineapples, papaya, guava, and soursop.

Crops for sale and eating

Many families have a small plot of land in the hills where they grow food for the table. Any extra crops are sold at market. This small-scale farming is called subsistence farming. Crops are also grown on a large scale for sale abroad. The most important of these "cash crops" are bananas, coffee, sugar cane, and tobacco.

◄ Coconut palms grow all over the Caribbean. Coconut milk is refreshing, and the flesh is used in many recipes.

Rice and peas

Rice and peas is a popular dish on islands such as Jamaica. The "peas" are really beans – usually red kidney beans. This recipe originally came from Africa.

RECIPE: rice and peas

Equipment
- large bowl • knife • cutting board • saucepan

Ingredients (serves four)
- 2 cups (450g) long-grain rice or brown rice
- 4 green onions • 1 green or red pepper
- 1¾ cups (400g) can kidney beans, including juice
- ¼ cup (50g) creamed coconut
- 1 sprig fresh thyme (or 1 teaspoon ground thyme)
- salt and pepper to taste
- small pat of butter or margarine

Ask a grown-up to help you with the chopping.

1 Wash the rice and soak it in a bowl of water. Meanwhile, finely chop the green onions and green or red pepper.

2 Boil 2 ½ cups (600ml) of water in a saucepan. Remove from heat and add the kidney beans and creamed coconut. Stir, then add all the other ingredients and stir again.

3 Cover the pan with a lid. Put it on the heat and simmer for 25–30 minutes until the rice is cooked and all the water is absorbed.

Meat and Seafood

Fish and shellfish have been important foods since the days of the Native Americans. The Spanish introduced livestock such as goats and chickens. Meat dishes such as curried goat are now local specialties, along with many seafood recipes.

◀ A dish of curried goat. Goats can be reared on land that is too steep, dry, or rocky for farming.

The Arawaks and Caribs hunted small mammals, ducks, lizards, and turtles. When the Spanish arrived in the 1500s, they brought chickens, pigs, goats, sheep, and cattle. These animals have been reared for their meat, milk, and eggs ever since. Goat, lamb, and other meats are barbecued, fried, or made into stews and curries. They form the basis of main meals and also delicious snacks.

Food from the sea

The Caribbean is famous for its seafood. Tuna and red snapper are among the fish you see displayed at markets. There are also more unusual catches – shark, marlin, flying fish, and barracuda. Shellfish such as prawns, lobster, conch, crabs, and crayfish are also harvested. Popular seafood

dishes include chowder (a rich soup) and prawns and rice. Fish and shellfish may be grilled, fried, curried, served jerk-style (see page 21), or made into cakes and patties. *Escovitch* fish is pickled according to a Spanish recipe.

Fishing grounds

The best fishing grounds in the Caribbean lie in the north, off the Bahamas and Cuba. Fish and shellfish netted in these waters are often sold abroad. Elsewhere, the small fish that abound around coral reefs provide food for homes and restaurants. Turtles and seal-like mammals called manatees are also caught, but these are now rare.

▲ A man cleans freshly caught snapper at a dockside market near Nassau in the Bahamas.

SALT FISH

The tradition of salting fish dates back to colonial times. Salt fish was often served to slaves, who had no chance to go fishing. Salted cod is featured in many recipes, including the traditional breakfast dish of salt fish and ackee (see page 17). Salt-fish fritters are called "stamp and go" in Jamaica.

What's Cooking?

Caribbean cooking is an incredibly varied blend of dishes from South America, Europe, West Africa, India, and China. Some recipes are hundreds of years old, while others are very recent. Caribbean food is sometimes called Creole cooking, which means a mix of European and African styles.

▲ Nutmeg fruits. The red spice visible inside one of them is called mace.

Dishes such as pepperpot stew were invented by the Arawaks. Pepperpot is a method of preserving meat using spices and cassava. Foo-foo (cassava or yam dumplings) and *coo-coo* (mashed cornmeal) come from Africa.

Hot and spicy

Caribbean food is very tasty because of all the spices that are used in cooking. Garlic, allspice, and hot chili peppers are native to these islands. Europeans brought spices from faraway places, such as nutmeg from Southeast Asia. Grenada is known for its nutmeg, which is even featured on the country's flag! West African food is often hot and peppery. Many Indian dishes use masala, a mixture of spices including coriander, cumin, mustard, and turmeric.

Through the day

Caribbean breakfasts are often very filling. Sweet and savory dishes, buns, and cakes may all be eaten at this time. Lunches can be quite light – such as a helping of pepperpot stew. Evening meals may turn into a banquet, with a starter, a main course with several vegetable dishes, followed by a sweet, sugary pudding or fresh fruit. The meal may be washed down with fruit juice, fresh lemonade, rum punch or ice-cold beer.

▼ Salt fish and ackee is the Jamaican national dish. It is often served with plantains.

ACKEE FOR BREAKFAST

Salt fish and ackee is the traditional breakfast dish on Jamaica. But it can also be eaten at other meals. Ackee is a red-skinned fruit from Africa. The yellow flesh inside looks and tastes quite like scrambled eggs when cooked!

Religion and Beliefs

Religion is part of everyday life in the Caribbean. People follow many different faiths and almost every island has its churches, mosques, and temples. Christianity is the most popular faith.

Christianity was introduced by Europeans in the 1500s and 1600s. On islands colonized by the French and Spanish, many people are Roman Catholics. On islands colonized by Britain, Anglicanism is more popular. There are also other Churches, such as Baptists and Pentecostalists. Church services are lively, with people singing and clapping to the music of guitars, cymbals, and drums. After mass on Sunday morning, people chat with friends and then go home to a big lunch.

▼ Followers of voodoo offer special foods, such as grilled corn, to their gods.

Asian and African faiths

Hinduism and Islam are important on islands such as Trinidad, which has a large Asian community. Other religions, such as Rastafarianism, began in the Caribbean itself (see panel). On Haiti, many people practice voodoo, a religion that blends Catholic and African beliefs.

RASTAFARIANISM

Rastafarianism began among the black community on Jamaica in the 1920s. It is now popular on many islands and also in other countries. Influenced by the Old Testament, Rastafarians identify the Caribbean with Babylon, the biblical land of exile and slavery for the Hebrew people. Rastafarians don't eat pork or shellfish. Many are vegetarian, and eat ital food – a vegetarian style of cooking. *Ital* means "natural."

▲ A Rastafarian reads from the Bible. Rastafarians eat pure foods. Many wear their hair in long plaits called dreadlocks.

Pocomania, practiced on Jamaica, also mixes Christian and African beliefs.

Religion and diet

Some religions have rules and customs concerning diet. Muslims don't eat pork or drink alcohol. Hindus don't eat beef, and many are vegetarian. During the Muslim month of fasting, Ramadan, Muslims fast from dawn to dusk, and only eat after dark. The end of Ramadan is marked by the feast of Id ul-Fitr.

Carnival Time

Carnival is the most famous Caribbean festival. It began as a Catholic festival, held just before Lent – the period of fasting before Easter. People celebrated before they gave up meat for Lent.

▲ Dancers perform during Carnival in Jacmel on Haiti.

Carnival was first celebrated on islands colonized by the French. It soon spread right across the Caribbean. African slaves added their own music and dances, and Asian people added bright colors and costumes.

Street parties

Carnival is party time in the Caribbean. People take to the streets in stunning costumes. Everyone marches and dances to the music of bands playing reggae, calypso, and other Caribbean music. Colorful floats move slowly through the crowded streets.

Carnival food

Stalls lining the streets sell many kinds of delicious foods, such as fried chicken, cakes, patties, and roti – an Indian flatbread filled with spicy meat or vegetables. The sizzle of jerk chicken fills the air. Jerk meat was invented by the Arawaks. Chicken, pork, or beef is steeped in a spicy sauce called a marinade, then grilled or barbecued.

RECIPE: jerk chicken

Equipment
- knife • cutting board • mixing bowl
- fork • shallow dish • baking tray • tongs

Ingredients (serves four)
- 6 green onions • 1 garlic clove
- 1 teaspoon (5 ml) ground allspice
- 1 tsp. (5 ml) ground cinnamon • 1 tsp. (5 ml) chili powder or paprika
- 2 tablespoons lime juice • 2 tablespoons olive oil
- 1 teaspoon soy sauce or vinegar
- 4 chicken pieces (or 8 drumsticks)
- salt and pepper to taste

Ask a grown-up to help you with the chopping and grilling. Beware of hot oil.

1 Finely chop the green onions and garlic. Put them in a bowl with the spices, lime juice and soy. Use a fork to mash them into a thick paste.

2 Place the chicken in a shallow dish. Spoon the paste over it. Cover with plastic wrap and refrigerate for at least 4 hours.

3 Place the chicken on a baking tray and sprinkle a little oil over it. Slowly grill the chicken for 15–20 minutes on each side. Turn using tongs. Make sure the meat is completely cooked.

Seasonal Celebrations

Celebrations take place throughout the year in the Caribbean. Every week at least one island has a carnival atmosphere, as a saint's day or another feast is celebrated. Along with Christian, Hindu, and Muslim holy days, there are also national days and sport and music festivals – and party food is always served!

◄ Stilt walkers and colorful dancers celebrate the festival of Crop Over on Barbados.

Crop Over

Late summer brings the harvest festival of Crop Over. This was originally held to celebrate the sugar cane harvest. On Barbados, there are parades, stilt-dancing, and singing competitions.

At this and most festivals, the traditional food is roast suckling pig. The animal is stuffed according to a secret recipe that varies from island to island, and then roasted slowly on a spit until the meat is very tender. You can also buy delicious snacks such as fried chicken, conch fritters and plantain, and sweet potato chips.

HINDU FESTIVALS

On Trinidad, Hindu festivals are public holidays. The spring festival of Phagwa is similar to Holi in India. There are parades, and people have fun throwing colored water over each other! Diwali, the festival of light, falls in autumn. All over Trinidad, little candles are lit to celebrate the victory of good over evil. People give presents and cards.

Saints days

On St Lucia, a fishing festival takes place on St Peter's Day in June. St Peter is the patron saint of fishermen. The brightly painted fishing boats are blessed and fish dishes such as salt-fish cakes are served.

On Puerto Rico, every town has its patron saint. Celebrations begin in church and spill out onto the streets with parades, music, and dancing. A king and queen are chosen from the costumed marchers. The festivities can continue for up to a week!

▼ Fish dishes are served at the festival of St Peter and St Paul on Dominica. Four out of five Dominicans are Catholic.

Christmas Time

Christmas and the New Year are celebrated Caribbean-style with parades, games, and feasting with special foods. On islands such as St Vincent and Montserrat, Christmas comes early, in mid-December, with celebrations lasting into the new year!

On Christmas Day, roast turkey, ham, suckling pig, or goat may be served. Side dishes of pumpkin and sweet potatoes are traditional. Christmas pudding and cake contain dried fruit such as currants and raisins steeped in rum. Cassava pie is eaten on Bermuda. People parade through the streets and let off homemade firecrackers. On Jamaica, Christmas carols are sung to a reggae beat.

Jonkonnu

Around this time, the festival of Jonkonnu is celebrated in Jamaica and the Bahamas. Costumed dancers with giant heads representing animals, devils, and other characters lead the parade. Bands of "set girls" with colored sashes dance to the music of pipes, whistles, and drums.

▶ Musicians wear colorful costumes during a Jonkonnu parade in the Bahamas.

Christmas drinks

Sorrel is a traditional Christmas drink made with dried sorrel flowers, oranges, and ginger. Some people drink rum-based cocktails. Tropical fruit punch is also popular.

RECIPE: tropical fruit punch

Equipment
- knife • cutting board • blender or sieve and spoon
- large pitcher • grater

Ingredients
- 1 large mango • 1¼ cup (300 ml) orange juice
- 1¼ cup (300 ml) pineapple juice
- ¾ cup (150 ml) lime juice • lemon or lime
- 1 teaspoon sugar or honey

Ask a grown-up to help you with the chopping.

1 Peel the mango. Cut a broad slice from both sides of the fruit first, then remove the other flesh.

2 Chop the mango into small pieces, then either mix it in a blender or mash it through a sieve using the back of a spoon.

3 Put the mango juice in a large pitcher. Grate the rind of a lime or lemon and add it with the other juices and sugar or honey.

4 Serve the punch in tall glasses with ice cubes or crushed ice. Decorate with slices of lemon or lime.

Island Specialties

Different islands in the Caribbean were colonized by the Spanish, French, English, Danish, and Dutch. Colonial influences are still evident in the language, culture, and cooking. In fact, you can almost guess an island's history from its food!

The Spanish were the first Europeans to settle in the Caribbean. They brought new foods such as onions, citrus fruit, sugar cane, and coconuts. On islands occupied by Spain, such as Cuba, Puerto Rico and Hispaniola, you will find Spanish dishes such as *arroz con camerones* (rice with prawns) and *escovitch* fish. Here and throughout the Caribbean, you will also find tasty African dishes made with yams, okra, beans, and cassava. In colonial times, every island had slaves, and now the majority of islanders are Afro-Caribbean.

◄ *Picadillo habanero* is a traditional dish of Cuba. It's a tasty beef hash made with tomato sauce, peppers, olives, capers, and garlic.

English rule

In the 1600s, the English took Jamaica from the Spanish. They also colonized the Bahamas, Barbados, Montserrat, and Antigua. The English introduced rum and the Cornish pasty, which became the Jamaican patty, filled with spicy meat, salt fish, or vegetables. Jamaican cooking also features dishes such as "dip and fall back," a stew with dumplings and bananas. "Mannish water" is spicy goat soup.

French and Dutch dishes

The French colonized Haiti, Guadeloupe, and Martinique. The last two are still part of France. French recipes, such as bouillabaisse (fish soup), chicken fricassée in coconut milk, and baked flamed bananas, are popular here. Another French speciality is frogs' legs, using the giant frogs of the Caribbean! The Dutch occupied Curacao, Bonaire, and Aruba in the Lesser Antilles. Dutch recipes include *erwensoep*, a thick pea soup.

▲ Goat stew is served on many islands, including Montserrat, shown here.

INDIAN COOKING

Trinidad is known for its Indian cooking. Dishes such as spicy lamb curry are cooked using a rich oil called ghee. Dhal puri is a popular snack. This is a flatbread made from chickpea flour, filled with curried meat and potatoes and then rolled up so you can eat it on the street.

Caribbean cooking is now enjoyed in lots of different countries – especially those with a big Caribbean community. In the last century, many people left the region to settle in Europe and North America.

Caribbean people often moved to countries with which they shared colonial ties. For example, there are over two million Puerto Ricans living in the United States, which took over Puerto Rico in 1898.

Sampling the cuisine

Many people get their first taste of Caribbean cooking while on vacation in the region. Or they may try it at home, at a Caribbean-style carnival. These carnivals take place in many cities with a sizeable Caribbean community – for example, London, Amsterdam, Toronto, New York, and Miami (see panel).

In these and other cities, Caribbean fruits and vegetables, such as yams and cassava, are now sold at markets. You can get ingredients such as creamed coconut at many supermarkets. There are also restaurants that specialize in Caribbean cuisine.

▶ Jerk chicken sizzles on a grill at the Notting Hill Carnival in London.

▲ Cuban dishes are served at a restaurant in the Little Havana section of Miami. This district has a large Cuban community and is named after the capital of Cuba.

CARIBBEAN FESTIVAL

The American city of Miami, Florida, has a large community of Cubans and other immigrants from Caribbean islands. Every year the city hosts the Calle Ocho festival, a Caribbean-style carnival with steel bands, floats, parades, and dancing. The delicious smell of Caribbean snacks such as jerk chicken, curried goat, and salt-fish fritters fills the air.

Western influence

Back in the Caribbean, Western foods such as hamburgers and french fries are now available in restaurants and fast-food outlets. These are enjoyed by locals, especially young people, as well as visitors. Big hotels in Caribbean resorts often serve Western food such as beef and tuna steaks. However, just a short distance away you can sample local cooking.

Something for everyone

The increasing popularity of Caribbean cooking is hardly surprising. After all, with so many flavors and dishes, there is something to suit everyone's taste!

Glossary

calypso A style of music that began in Trinidad.

cash crop A crop that is grown for sale, often for sale abroad.

colonial Relating to a colony.

colonize Establish a colony in another country or place.

colony A country that is ruled by another country.

cuisine The cooking of a region or of a particular group of people.

democracy A form of government in which the people elect representatives to rule on their behalf.

fricassée Describes pieces of stewed or fried meat served in a thick, white sauce.

immigrant A person who comes to a country and settles there.

indentured worker A person who signs a contract to work for a certain number of years, usually for low pay.

introduce Bring something, such as new types of plants or animals, somewhere for the first time.

marinade A sauce in which fish, meat, or another food is soaked before cooking to give it extra flavor and tenderness.

plantation A large area of land used to grow a single crop.

plate One of the huge slabs of rock that make up the Earth's outer crust. These are also known as tectonic plates.

reggae A form of music invented in Jamaica. Reggae has a strong, regular beat.

republic A form of government without a king or queen. People usually elect the government, which is often headed by a president.

roti A flatbread used in Indian cooking.

staple food A food that forms the basis of the diet of the people in a particular country or region.

subsistence farming When crops are grown mainly to feed the farmer's family.

sugar mill A factory in which sugar cane is processed to make sugar.

terraced Describes a hillside that has been cut into flat steps for farming.

trade winds The prevailing (main) winds that blow in the tropics.

tropics The region on either side of the equator.

vegetarian (1) A type of cooking that does not use meat or fish. (2) A person who does not eat meat or fish.

Further Information

Books

Caribbean Cooking by Jane Hartshorn (Parragon, 1996)

The Changing Face of the Caribbean by Ali Brownlie (Wayland, 2002)

Cooking Around the World: Cooking the Caribbean Way by Cheryl Davidson Kaufman (Lerner, 2009)

Country File: The Caribbean by Ian Graham (Franklin Watts, 2005)

Food and Festivals: The Caribbean by Linda Illsley (Wayland, 2001)

Traditions from the Caribbean by Paul Dash (Wayland, 1998)

Websites

www.bbc.co.uk/caribbean/
BBC site on the Caribbean.

www.foodbycountry.com/Algeria-to-France/Cuba.html
Food in Cuba: General information about Cuba and recipes.

www.geographia.com/indx02.htm
Facts about Caribbean islands.

go.hrw.com/atlas/norm_htm/caribean.htm
Maps of the Caribbean.

Index

Page numbers in **bold** refer to pictures.